Dear Parent:
Your child's love of reading

D1296170

child learns to read in a different way and at h... can help your young reader improve and beco... confident by encouraging his or her own interests and abilities. You can also guide your child's spiritual development by reading stories with biblical values and Bible stories, like I Can Read! books published by Zonderkidz. From books your child reads with you to the first books he or she reads alone, there are I Can Read! books for every stage of reading:

SHARED READING
Basic language, word repetition, and whimsical illustrations, ideal for sharing with your emergent reader.

BEGINNING READING
Short sentences, familiar words, and simple concepts for children eager to read on their own.

READING WITH HELP
Engaging stories, longer sentences, and language play for developing readers.

READING ALONE
Complex plots, challenging vocabulary, and high-interest topics for the independent reader.

ADVANCED READING
Short paragraphs, chapters, and exciting themes for the perfect bridge to chapter books.

I Can Read! books have introduced children to the joy of reading since 1957. Featuring award-winning authors and illustrators and a fabulous cast of beloved characters, I Can Read! books set the standard for beginning readers.

A lifetime of disc... **Can Read!"**

Visit www.icanread.... ading experience.
Visit www.... d! titles.

TIGARD PUBLIC LIBRARY
13500 SW HALL BLVD
TIGARD OR 97223-8111
A member of Washington County
Cooperative Library Services
WITHDRAWN

Bear with each other and forgive
whatever grievances you may have against one another.
Forgive as the Lord forgave you.
—Colossians 3:13

To Jen, Dave, Ellie, and Cassie
–D.D.M.

ZONDERKIDZ

Bob's Great Escape
Copyright © 2011 by Dandi Daley Mackall
Illustrations copyright © 2011 by Claudia Wolf

Requests for information should be addressed to:
Zonderkidz, *Grand Rapids, Michigan 49530*

Library of Congress Cataloging-in-Publication Data

Mackall, Dandi Daley.

Bob's great escape / by Dandi Daley Mackall ; illustrated by Claudia Wolf.
p. cm. — (Horse named Bob)
Summary: When Bob the horse disappears from his pasture and Mrs. Gray accuses Jen of having left the gate open, Jen has a hard time forgiving her for not believing the truth.
ISBN 978-0-310-71784-3 (softcover)
[1. Horses—Fiction. 2. Lost and found possessions—Fiction. 3. Forgiveness—Fiction. 4. Christian life—Fiction.] I. Wolf, Claudia, ill. II. Title.
PZ7.M1905Bob 2011
[E]—dc22 2009037512

All Scripture quotations unless otherwise noted are taken from the Holy Bible, *New International Version®, NIV®*. Copyright © 1973, 1978, 1984 by Biblica, Inc.™ Used by permission of Zondervan. All rights reserved worldwide.

Any Internet addresses (websites, blogs, etc.) and telephone numbers printed in this book are offered as a resource. They are not intended in any way to be or imply an endorsement by Zondervan, nor does Zondervan vouch for the content of these sites and numbers for the life of this book.

All rights reserved. No part of this publication may be reproduced, stored in a retrieval system, or transmitted in any form or by any means—electronic, mechanical, photocopy, recording, or any other—except for brief quotations in printed reviews, without the prior permission of the publisher.

Zonderkidz is a trademark of Zondervan.

Printed in China

11 12 13 14 15/SCC/ 7 6 5 4 3 2 1

8643

Bob's Great Escape

story by Dandi Daley Mackall

pictures by Claudia Wolf

“Let’s ride to the park,”

Jen said to her friend Dave.

“Great!” Dave said.

Dave was riding his pony, Lily.

Jen was riding Bob the Horse.

Mrs. Gray let Jen ride Bob.

Jen took care of the big horse.

Bob stopped at the park.

He tried to eat the nice park grass.

“Why does he do that?” Dave asked.

Jen pulled Bob away from the grass.

“Bob thinks grass is greener on the other side of the fence,” Jen said.

Jen and Dave rode home.

Jen took Bob back

to Mrs. Gray.

Then Jen cleaned her room.

“Time for lunch!” Mom said.

Jen ate lunch, but she missed Bob.

"I'm going over to see Bob again,"

Jen told Mom.

Jen walked to Mrs. Gray's yard.

But she didn't see Bob.

“Here, Bob!” Jen called.

Mrs. Gray came outside.

“Where’s Bob?” Jen asked.

“How should I know?”

said Mrs. Gray. “You rode him.”

Jen called and called, “Here, Bob!”

But Bob wasn’t there.

“He’s gone, Bob’s gone!” Jen cried.

“Look at this!” Mrs. Gray shouted.

Jen ran over and looked.

The gate to Bob's pen was wide open.

"Look what you did!" said Mrs. Gray.

"You left the gate open."

“I closed that gate,” Jen said.

“No, you did not!” Mrs. Gray said.

“I better go call for help.”

Jen began to cry. “I did close it,” she said. “You have to believe me.”

Jen, Mom, and Dad looked for Bob.

They tried Dave's yard.

"She's not with Lily," Dave said.

They looked across
the road.

They looked in
the barn.

Jen prayed Bob would be okay.
She prayed they would find him soon.
"Poor Bob," Jen said.
"We have to find him."

“I did close that gate,” Jen said.

“We believe you,” Dad said.

“Mrs. Gray doesn’t,” Jen said.

Jen was sad. But she was mad too.

“It’s just not fair!” she said.

“You need to forgive her,” Mom said.

“How can I do that?” Jen asked.

“Think like Mrs. Gray,” Dad said.

“Maybe you can understand her.”

“I don’t want to think
like Mrs. Gray,” Jen said.
“I’d rather think like Bob.”
That gave Jen an idea.

“Okay. I’m Bob the Horse,”

Jen said. “Where do I want to go?

That’s it!” Jen shouted. “Come on!”

“There you are, Bob!” Jen shouted.

“I knew you would be at the park!”

“How did you know?” Mom asked.

“I had to think like Bob,” Jen said.

“He thinks grass is greener here.”

Jen led Bob back to Mrs. Gray's.

"Lock the gate this time, Jen!"

Mrs. Gray said.

Jen started to talk back to her.

Then she tried to think like

Mrs. Gray.

Jen put Bob in and locked the gate.

"I know you were worried," Jen said.

"I was worried too, Mrs. Gray."

“Hey! Look at that!” Mrs. Gray said.

Jen turned to see Bob at the gate.

He pushed the lock with his nose.

The gate opened.

Jen ran up and closed the gate.

"You opened it yourself!" she said.

"I'm sorry for thinking you did it,"
Mrs. Gray told Jen.
"I understand," Jen said.
"You were just worried."
"That's true," Mrs. Gray said.
"How did you get to be so smart?"

Jen grinned at Bob the Horse.

"I learned to think like a horse."